Paddington Does the Decorating

written by *Michael Bond*
illustrated by *Nick Ward for Ross Design*

Young Lions
An Imprint of HarperCollins*Publishers*

First published in Great Britain 1993 in Young Lions
3 5 7 9 8 6 4 2

Young Lions is an imprint of the Children's Division,
part of HarperCollins Publishers Ltd,
77–85 Fulham Palace Road, Hammersmith,
London W6 8JB

Text copyright © Michael Bond 1993
Illustrations copyright © HarperCollins Publishers Ltd 1993

Adapted from *A Spot of Decorating* from *More About Paddington*
Text copyright © Michael Bond 1957
Available in Young Lions

The author asserts the moral right to be
identified as the author of this work

ISBN 0 00 674674-8

Printed and bound in Great Britain by
HarperCollins Manufacturing, Glasgow

Part One

Paddington gave a deep sigh and pulled his hat down over his ears to keep out the noise. There was such a hullabaloo going on, it was difficult to write in his scrapbook.

Mr and Mrs Brown had received an unexpected invitation to a wedding. Paddington wasn't going - he didn't really like weddings.

But he was beginning to wish that everyone would hurry up and go. He had a special reason for wanting to be alone.

He sighed again and wiped the pen carefully on the back of his paw.

Then he mopped up some ink blots which had found their way on to the table.

At that moment, the door burst open and Mrs Brown rushed in.

Paddington stuck his tongue out as far as he could.

"It *is* a funny colour," he said, squinting down at it. "Perhaps I'm sickening for something!"

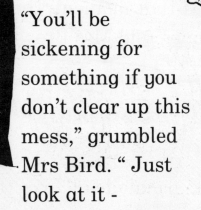

"You'll be sickening for something if you don't clear up this mess," grumbled Mrs Bird. " Just look at it -

bottles of ink,

6

glue,

bits of paper,

my best
sewing scissors,

marmalade all over the place,

and goodness knows what else."

Paddington looked around. It *was*
in a bit of a state.

"I've almost finished," he announced. "I've got to rule more lines and things. I've been writing my memories."

Paddington took his scrapbook very seriously and spent many long hours carefully pasting in pictures and writing up his adventures.

Well, make sure you clear everything up. Take care of yourself.

The Browns waved goodbye.

"Perhaps I ought to stay,"
said Mr Brown.
He didn't like
weddings either.
" I could finish
decorating
his room."

"I'm sure
Paddington will be
perfectly happy
by himself,"
said Mrs Brown.

"I dare say he'll be *happy*," said Mrs Bird. "It's what he's likely to get up to that bothers me."

Part Two

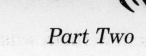

In his scrapbook, Paddington
wrote the words:

At a lewse end

Paddington was beginning to get
impatient. His belongings had
been packed away for a long time,
ready for the big move to his
new room.

Every time he wanted anything
special, he had to undo yards and
yards of string and brown paper.

Paddington's new room was a sore
point in the Browns' household.
It was over two weeks since Mr
Brown had started decorating it.
He had stripped all the old
wallpaper from the walls;

taken off
the wood
round
the door,

the door handle,

and everything else that was loose
(or that he had made loose),

and bought a lot of bright new
wallpaper, some whitewash and
some paint.

Then he had left it.

Paddington had offered to help
with the decorating several times,
but Mr Brown hadn't even allowed
him in the room.

Paddington had an

He scratched out 'At a lewse end'
from his scrapbook and wrote

Then he
cleared everything
up, locked his scrapbook
carefully in his suitcase
and hurried upstairs.

Part Three

Paddington went into his new
room and carefully closed the door
behind him.

He sniffed. There was an exciting
smell of paint and whitewash,

some steps,

a trestle table,

several brushes,

some rolls
of wallpaper

and a big bucket of whitewash.

The room had a lovely echo as well,
and he spent a long time sitting in
the middle of the floor, stirring the
paint and listening to his new
voice.

TRA LA LA LAA?

Paddington decided to paint first.
He chose one of Mr Brown's
best brushes, dipped it
into the pot of paint,

and looked round the room for
something to dab it on.

He started on the window frame.

After a while, his arm began to ache. He tried dipping his paw in the paint pot and rubbing the paint on.

But more paint seemed to go on the glass than the wood. The room became quite dark.

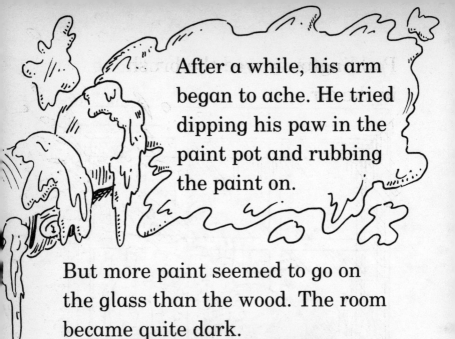

I wish I'd started on something else.

Paddington waved the brush
in the air.

Perhaps if
I whitewash
the ceiling, I
can cover all the
drips on the
wall with the
wallpaper.

But Paddington discovered that whitewashing was almost as hard as painting.

Even standing on tip-toe at the top of the steps, he found it hard to reach the ceiling.

The bucket of whitewash
was much too heavy for
him to lift so he had
to run down the
steps every time
he dipped his
brush in.

When he carried his brush up
again, the whitewash ran down his
paw on to his fur.

Things were
getting in rather
a mess.

Then Paddington had a brainwave.

There was a house being built
nearby. He had spent many hours
talking to the builders and
watching them. They had a rope
and pulley to hoist their tools and
cement up to the top floor.

He looked up. There was a hook in the middle of the ceiling where a lamp used to hang.

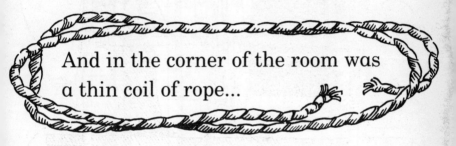

And in the corner of the room was a thin coil of rope...

Paddington set to work quickly. First, he tied one end of the rope to the bucket.

This should do the trick.

Then he climbed
up the steps and
passed the other
end through the
hook in the ceiling. It took him a
long time. The bucket was full of
whitewash and very heavy.

At the top of the rope, things started to go wrong. Paddington closed his eyes and leaned back for the last pull.

Suddenly, he felt as if he was floating.

He opened his eyes and saw —

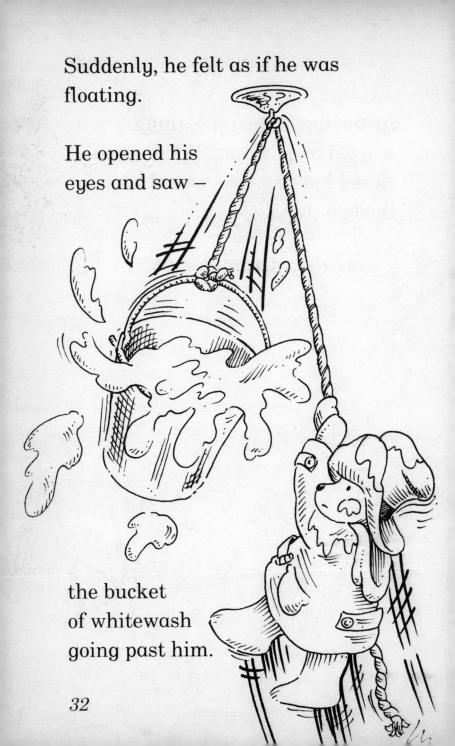

the bucket
of whitewash
going past him.

Paddington looked down. The whitewash was running out of the bucket. As the bucket got lighter, the rope moved again.

Paddington landed with a

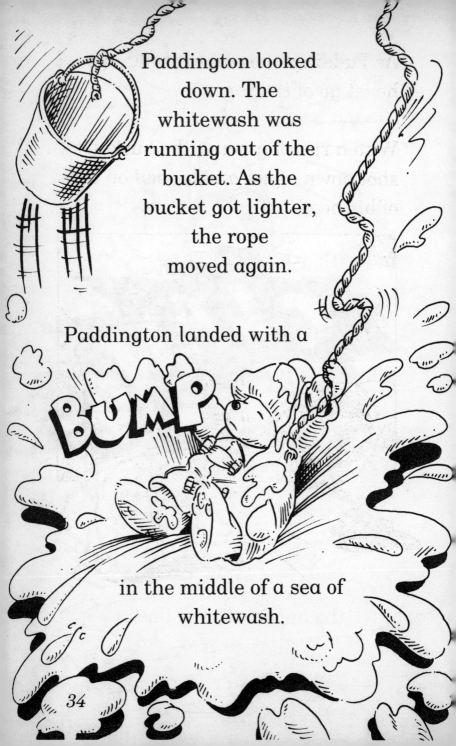

BUMP

in the middle of a sea of whitewash.

As Paddington tried to stand up,
he let go of the rope.

With a rushing noise, the bucket
shot down again and landed on top
of his head.

Part Four

Paddington sat up and took the bucket off his head.

He quickly put it back on again. There was whitewash all over the floor. The paint pots had been

upset into little rivers of brown and green.

Mr Brown's decorating cap was floating in one corner of the room.

He was going to have a lot of explaining to do – and he wasn't even sure what had gone wrong.

It was then that he had another idea.

If he did the wallpapering very well, the others might not even notice the mess.

Paddington had often watched Mr Brown through a crack in the door. He thought wallpapering looked quite simple.

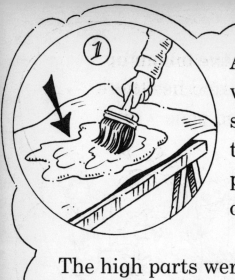

All you had to do was brush some sticky stuff on the back of the paper and put it on the wall.

The high parts weren't too difficult because you folded the paper in two and put a broom where the fold was.

Then you pushed the broom up and down the wall in case there were any wrinkles.

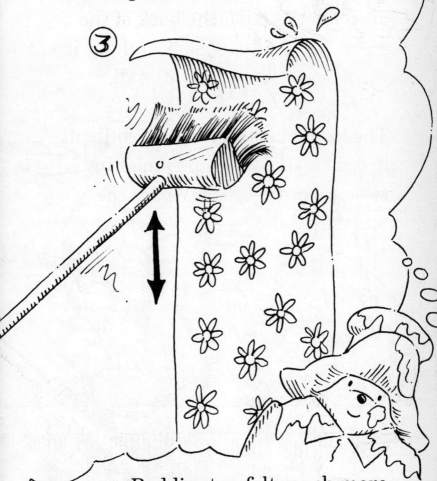

Paddington felt much more cheerful.

He found some paste already
mixed in another bucket. He put it
on top of the trestle while he
unrolled the paper.

Every time he tried to unroll the paper, he had to crawl along the table, pushing it with his paws.

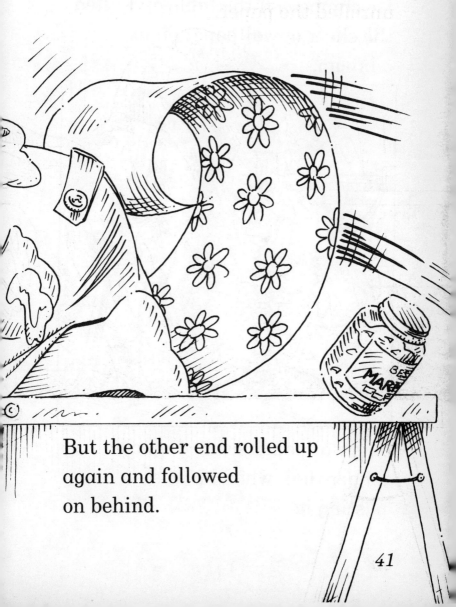

But the other end rolled up again and followed on behind.

41

At last he managed to get one
piece covered in paste.

He climbed off the table and lifted
the sheet of wallpaper on to
a broom.

The wallpaper seemed much
longer than when he was
pasting it.

Somehow, it began
to wrap itself
around him.

After a struggle, he managed to
push his way out and headed
towards the wall.

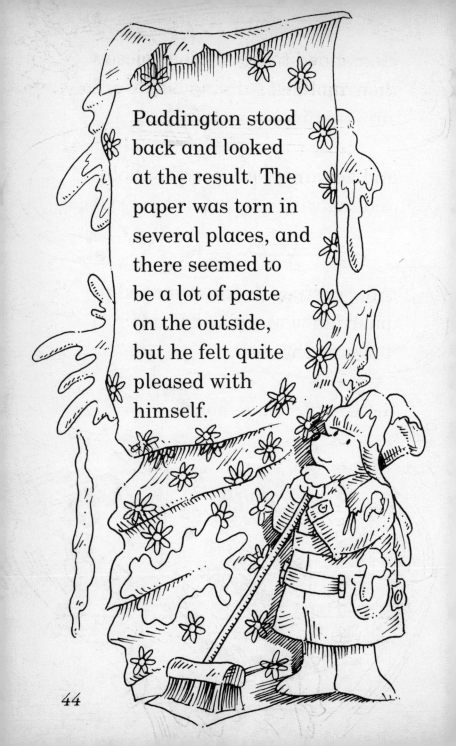

Paddington stood back and looked at the result. The paper was torn in several places, and there seemed to be a lot of paste on the outside, but he felt quite pleased with himself.

He decided to try another piece,
then another, running backwards

and forwards between the table
and the walls as fast as his legs

could carry him. He was
determined to finish before

the Browns came home.

45

Some of the pieces
didn't quite join,

others overlapped,

and there were some very odd-
looking patches of paste and
whitewash.

None of the pieces were as straight as he would have liked.

But when he put his head on one side and squinted, the overall effect was quite nice. He felt very pleased with himself.

As Paddington looked round the
room, he noticed something
strange.

There was a window,

and a fireplace.

But there was no sign of a door.

Paddington stopped squinting and his eyes grew rounder and rounder.

He remembered there *had* been a door, because he had come through it. He blinked at all four walls.

It was difficult to see properly
because the paint on the window
glass had started to dry and there
was hardly any light coming
through - but there definitely
wasn't a door.

Part Five

"I can't understand it," said Mr Brown. " I've looked everywhere and there's no sign of Paddington. I told you I should have stayed at home with him."

Mrs Brown looked worried. "Oh dear, I hope nothing's happened to him. It's so unlike him to go out without leaving a note."

"He's not in his room," said Judy.

Mrs Bird came in with the supper.

Have _you_ seen Paddington anywhere?

I don't know about Paddington. I've had enough trouble over the water pipes without missing bears. Those pipes have been banging away since we came in.

PADDINGTON

They burst through the papered-up door.

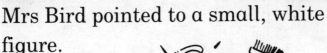

> There must have been an earthquake or something. And either that's Paddington or it's his ghost.

Mrs Bird pointed to a small, white figure.

"I couldn't find the door," said Paddington. "I think I must have papered over it when I did the decorating. It was there when I came in. I remember seeing it. So I banged on the floor with a broom handle."

"Gosh. What a mess!" said
Jonathan.

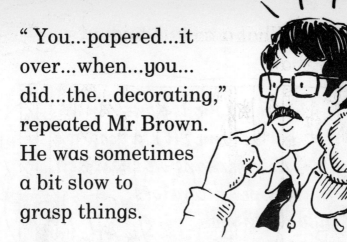

" You...papered...it over...when...you...did...the...decorating," repeated Mr Brown. He was sometimes a bit slow to grasp things.

That's right Mr Brown. I did it as a surprise.

Paddington waved a paw round the room. "I'm afraid it's in a bit of a mess. It isn't dry yet."

Mrs Bird came to Paddington's rescue.

What's done is done. And if you ask me, it's a good job too. Now perhaps we shall get some proper decorators in to do the job.

PLIP
PLOP

She took hold of Paddington's paw and led him out of the room.

Mr Brown looked at the long trail
of white footprints and paw-marks.

"Bears!" he said, bitterly.

After his bath, Paddington hung about in his room for a long time, and waited until the last possible moment before going downstairs to supper. He had a nasty feeling he was in disgrace. But surprisingly, nobody mentioned the word 'decorating' that evening.

When he was sitting up
in bed with his cocoa,
Paddington was even more
surprised that several people
came to see him - and each of
them gave him ten pence.

It was all very mysterious.

Judy solved the problem when she came to say goodnight.

"Oh no you don't," said Judy sternly. "You've done quite enough for one day. If I were you, I shouldn't mention the word 'decorating' for a long time to come."

Paddington stretched out his paws. "Perhaps you're right," he said. "But I *was* at a loose end."